MARY WRIGHTLY, SO POLITELY

SHIRIN YIM BRIDGES

ILLUSTRATED BY
MARIA MONESCILLO

HARCOURT CHILDREN'S BOOKS
Houghton Mifflin Harcourt
Boston   New York 2013

Text copyright © 2013 by Shirin Yim Bridges
Illustrations copyright © 2013 by Maria Monescillo

Harcourt Children's Books
is an imprint of Houghton Mifflin Harcourt Publishing Company.

www.hmhbooks.com

The text in this book was set in Aged Book.
The display type was set in 1786 GLC Fournier Caps.
The illustrations were done in pastel on cardboard with digital retouching.
Design by Christine Kettner

LIBRARY OF CONGRESS CATALOGING-IN-PUBLICATION DATA

Bridges, Shirin Yim
Mary Wrightly, so politely / by Shirin Bridges ; illustrated by Maria Monescillo.
p. cm.
Summary: Mary Wrightly is a polite young girl who speaks in a small, soft voice—
unless she really wants to be heard!—Provided by publisher.
ISBN 978-0-547-34248-1
[1. Etiquette—Fiction. 2. Assertiveness (Psychology)—Fiction.] I. Monescillo, Maria, ill. II. Title.
PZ7.B76197Mar 2013
[E]—dc23
2012019633
Manufactured in China
SCP 10 9 8 7 6 5 4 3 2 1
4500393675

To the Bear, for appreciating my small voice. —S.Y.B.

For Marcos. I finally found you. —M.M.

M ARY WRIGHTLY was a good, polite little girl who spoke in a small, soft voice. Whenever she asked for something, Mary Wrightly would, so politely, say "Please." She always, so politely, said "Thank you," and sometimes even "Thank you very much."

Mary's voice was so small and soft, she often had to say things more than once.

"My name is Mary and I have a baby brother," Mary said softly.

"Mary, please speak up," said her teacher.

Mary tried.

"My name is Mary and I have a baby brother," she said just a little louder.

When Mary's baby brother was nearly a year old, Mary asked her mother
to take her to the toy store. She wanted to buy him a birthday present.

On the bus, Mary Wrightly gave
her seat to an old lady.
"Thank you," said the old lady.
"You're welcome," said Mary Wrightly,
so politely.

She didn't complain when a boy
stepped on her toe. In fact,
Mary Wrightly, so politely,
said, "I'm sorry."

When Mary and her mother reached the toy store, it was very crowded.
They had to squeeze themselves in the door—and who did they find inside
but their neighbor, Mrs. Giles.

As her mother and Mrs. Giles chatted, Mary waited, trying to keep out of everybody's way. "Ooof, excuse me!" said Mary Wrightly, so politely, as a handbag bonked her on the head.

"Oh, I'm sorry," said Mary Wrightly, so politely, squashing herself against a shelf to let a man pass.

That's when Mary spotted a teddy bear. It was the perfect gift for her baby brother. But just as she reached for it . . .

. . . a pair of hands whisked it away.

"Excuse me," said Mary Wrightly, so politely.

But the girl simply walked off with the teddy bear.

Mary knew it was not polite to sulk. With a little sigh,
she looked around. Up on the highest shelf,
she spotted a fluffy duck.

"Excuse me, Mama,"
said Mary Wrightly, so politely.
She took her mother's hand
and gave it a little squeeze.
"Mama, there's a duck up there," she said.
But before her mother could look . . .

. . . the duck was gone.

Mary knew that it was not polite to sulk.
And Mary knew that making a scene was even worse.
So she bit her bottom lip and blinked back
her disappointment.

"Don't worry, Mary," said her mother.

"We'll find something else for your brother."

Then she went back to talking to Mrs. Giles.

But now, when Mary looked around, the shelves were no longer full of toys.

"Mama . . . " said Mary Wrightly, so politely, and this time she tugged her mother's hand.

"Just one more second, Mary," said her mother.

That's when Mary turned and saw it.

The little blue elephant had round, pink cheeks just like the elephants

Mary and her mother had carefully painted on the walls of her brother's room.

And it had a sweet smile, like her baby brother.

But just as she reached for it . . .

. . . a lady stepped up and took it.

"Excuse me," said Mary Wrightly, so politely.

"Excuse me!"

Mary said a little louder.

"Excuse me,
but that blue elephant
is for
my baby brother!"

"Oh," said the lady. "I'm so sorry." She handed the elephant to Mary.

"Thank you," said Mary Wrightly, so politely. "And I'm sorry for raising my voice."

"That's quite all right," said the lady. "I didn't see you there. I'm sure your brother will like this elephant very much."

"Thank you," repeated Mary Wrightly.

Her mother knelt beside her. "I think it's perfect!" she said.

So Mary took the blue elephant home on the bus.

"That's a lovely elephant," said an old gentleman.

"Thank you very much, sir," said Mary Wrightly, so politely.

"Can I see that elephant?" asked a little girl.

"Of course," said Mary Wrightly, so politely.

"It's a birthday present for my baby brother."

At home, Mary ran straight to her brother's room
and dangled the blue elephant over his crib.
The elephant smiled down at her baby brother.
Her baby brother smiled up at the elephant.

"Happy birthday! I really hope you like it,"
said Mary Wrightly, so politely.

"Maaagaaagaaa!"

said her baby brother.